PICKY PEGGY

by Jennifer Dussling
illustrated by Lynn Adams

Kane Press, Inc.
New York

Thanks to Roberta Giblin for sharing the story of Joe, Chris, Patty, and their duck.—J. K. & J. D.

Acknowledgements: Our thanks to Dr. Susan Roberts, Professor of Nutrition at Tufts University and author of Feeding Your Child for Lifelong Health and William F. Dean, Ph.D., former Researcher and Director, Cornell University Duck Research Laboratory, for helping us make this book as accurate as possible.

Library of Congress Cataloging-in-Publication Data

Dussling, Jennifer.
  Picky Peggy / by Jennifer Dussling ; illustrated by Lynn Adams.
    p. cm. — (Science solves it!)
Summary: Peggy, who is known for being a picky eater, decides to become "Peggy the bold eater" after learning a lesson from her pet duckling.
  ISBN: 978-57565-138-5 (pbk. : alk. paper)
  [1. Food habits—Fiction. 2. Nutrition—Fiction. 3. Ducks—Fiction. 4. Animals—Infancy—Fiction.] I. Adams, Lynn (Lynn Joan), ill. II. Title. III. Series.
  PZ7.D943Pi 2004
  [E]—dc22

2003012855

10 9 8 7 6 5 4

First published in the United States of America in 2003 by Kane Press, Inc.
Printed at Worzalla Publishing, Stevens Point, WI, U.S.A., February 2010

Science Solves It! is a registered trademark of Kane Press, Inc.

Book Design/Art Direction: Edward Miller

www.kanepress.com

"Are they here yet?" Peggy called.

"Yes," Mr. Cooper said. "Come and see."

"Yay!" Peggy yelled, and scrambled over the fence.

There they were. One, two, three, four, five—
six of them! Six brand-new, just-hatched baby
ducks! They were yellow and fluffy with black
eyes and orange beaks and feet. They were the
cutest things Peggy had ever seen!

"Which one is mine?" Peggy asked.

"You choose," Mr. Cooper said.

Peggy looked and looked. Finally she chose the fluffiest duck of all. "I'm going to call him Fluff," she said.

"That's a good name for such a fluffy duck," Mr. Cooper told her.

Mr. Cooper gave Peggy a bag of duck food that he had made himself. He told her to give Fluff plenty of water to drink and some other foods, like veggies. "Keep him warm," Mr. Cooper said. "And don't let him swim just yet."

"Don't worry, Mr. Cooper," said Peggy. "I'll take good care of Fluff."

Peggy played with Fluff all day long. He liked to shake his wings and waddle across the floor. That always made Peggy laugh. Sometimes they blew bubbles together. Sometimes they had tea parties. They didn't drink tea, though. They drank water.

How are you and Peggy and Fluff alike? You all need water—and lots of it—to stay healthy.

Peggy gave Fluff some duck food and some bread crumbs. She had fed bread crumbs to Mr. Cooper's ducks lots of times. Fluff liked the bread crumbs. He liked them even better than his duck food.

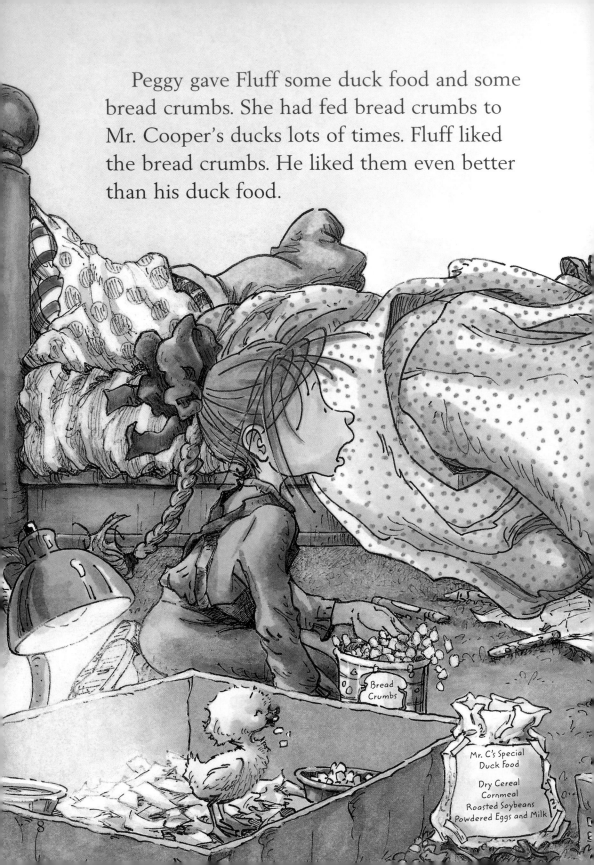

Bread Crumbs

Mr. C's Special Duck Food

Dry Cereal
Cornmeal
Roasted Soybeans
Powdered Eggs and Milk

"Peggy, it's time for dinner," her mom said.

"Do I have to eat?" Peggy asked. "I'm having fun with Fluff."

"Peggy Elizabeth Sullivan," her mother said.

"Uh-oh," said Peggy. "We'd better go, Fluff."

Peggy sat down and looked at her plate. Yuck! Fish and green beans and mashed potatoes. "Eat up, Peggy," her dad said. "You're a growing girl."

Peggy was a picky eater. In fact, Peggy was proud of how picky she was. Her brother, Mark, didn't like broccoli. Her sister, Valerie, didn't like eggs. But Peggy hardly liked anything.

She didn't like broccoli, or eggs, or milk, or meat, or potatoes, or soup. And she *hated* spinach. She didn't like the way it looked, or the way it felt in her mouth, or the way it tasted.

The only thing Peggy really liked for dinner was noodles with butter.

Different foods have different vitamins and minerals that help you grow and stay healthy. For example, carrots and broccoli have vitamin A. Oranges and green peppers have vitamin C. Milk and cheese have calcium. And spinach—Peggy's least favorite food—has iron and vitamin A.

The rest of the family had finished dinner. But Peggy still sat at the table looking at her food. Now and then Fluff quacked. Peggy could tell he felt bad for her.

Finally her mom gave in—kind of. "Eat some fish and green beans," she said. "Then I'll make noodles for you."

Peggy took just a mouthful of fish and three green beans. But she ate *all* the noodles.

"When I have kids, they won't have to eat the
stuff they don't like!" Peggy told Fluff.

She poured some bread crumbs into her hand
for him. "You like bread crumbs best," she went
on. "So you can have all you want. You don't have
to eat duck food or veggies or anything else."

Fluff quacked. Peggy could tell he liked
the idea.

Peggy played with Fluff every day. She read
books to him. She patted his soft feathers. She
splashed him with water.

Fluff followed Peggy everywhere. He even
followed her into the bathroom!

A week went by and Peggy took Fluff to
visit his brothers and sisters. They were getting
big. They seemed bigger than Fluff. But maybe
that didn't matter. Maybe Fluff was just small
for his age.

Peggy tried to take even better care of Fluff. She petted him and sang to him and gave him plenty of water and bread crumbs.

But Fluff still looked small. And he didn't seem so happy anymore.

Another week went by, and Peggy got a call from Mr. Cooper. "I'm letting the ducks outside for the first time," he told her. "Bring Fluff over."

"We'll be right there!" said Peggy.

As soon as Peggy and Fluff arrived, Mr. Cooper went to the shed. He opened the door. One by one, the ducks came out. They wiggled their feathers. They tilted their heads up to the sunshine. They quacked and waddled around the yard.

Fluff stood off to the side. He was quiet and still. That's when Peggy got worried.

Fluff didn't look like the other ducks anymore. They had shiny feathers and bright eyes. His feathers were droopy. His eyes didn't sparkle. Fluff didn't look like a ball of fluff anymore.

"Something is wrong with Fluff!" Peggy said.

"You're right," said Mr. Cooper. He picked up Fluff. He looked at his eyes and his feet and his feathers. "What are you feeding him?" he asked.

"Bread crumbs," Peggy said.

"Didn't he like the duck food?" asked Mr. Cooper.

FOOD FOR THOUGHT!
The right food is good for your brain. It makes your bones and muscles strong and keeps your skin, eyes, hair, and teeth healthy.

"Bread crumbs are his favorite," Peggy explained. "So that's what I give him."

"Ducks need more than bread crumbs to be healthy," Mr. Cooper said. "A growing duck should eat other food, too—like spinach, and carrots, and fruit, and cheese."

Peggy made a face. "Spinach? Carrots? Yuck!"

"Just watch," Mr. Cooper said. He went into the shed and came back with a dish of food. Fluff started eating. He ate and ate.

Peggy looked in the dish. The food was red and orange. It was tomatoes and mashed carrots. And Fluff liked it!

Did you eat a rainbow today?
Here's a trick to be sure you're eating healthy.
Think color! Every day try to eat as many different colored fruits and veggies as you can—red, orange, yellow, purple, dark green, and light green.

"Sometimes what a pet likes best is not the best thing for it," Mr. Cooper explained. "They're not so different from people."

He said Fluff would be better in no time once he started eating the right things.

Too much sugar and salt is not good for you. Be careful with sweets and chips. A little is okay— a lot is not!

As soon as Peggy got home, she fed Fluff
some of the duck food. He ate it all up.

Later on she gave him some watermelon,
cheese, and spinach. Fluff ate all the watermelon
and cheese—but he didn't eat the spinach.
Peggy smiled. Fluff didn't like spinach, either!

At dinner that night, Peggy's mom put a plate in front of her—meatloaf, peas, and rice.

Peggy thought about what Mr. Cooper had said.

She thought about Fluff's droopy feathers. She thought about his dull eyes. *She* didn't want to look dull and droopy. She picked up her fork and took a bite of the peas.

"Mom!" Mark yelled. "Look! Peggy's eating!"
"Leave her alone," her mother said.
Valerie and Mark watched Peggy eat her meatloaf, and her peas, and her rice. She drank her milk, too.

"Does this mcan you'll eat anything?" Valerie asked. "Even fish, and broccoli, and eggs?"

Peggy nodded. She could tell Valerie and Mark were impressed. That made her feel good. In fact, it gave her an idea.

You get energy from the food you eat. It's like putting gasoline in a car. So, fill up with the best kinds of food to keep healthy and strong!

She wouldn't be Peggy the picky eater any
more. She'd be Peggy the bold eater! She'd eat
all kinds of fancy foods—like fried mushrooms
and brown mustard and the little Chinese corn
that comes in salads! Everyone would be so
amazed.

"Will you even eat spinach?" Mark asked.

Peggy thought about it—the limp green leaves, the slimy feel in her mouth, and the sour taste. "I'll eat fish, and meat, and eggs, and milk, and broccoli, and peas," she said. "But I *can't* eat spinach!"

Fluff quacked. He probably felt the same way!

Fluff the **Bold** Eater
Ducks eat things that Peggy shouldn't even try, things like garden snails, slugs, bugs, and earthworms!

Neither Peggy nor Fluff ever did eat spinach. But every day they had a snack—and they ate it together. Sometimes it was fruit. Sometimes it was popcorn. Sometimes it was vegetables.

And sometimes Peggy and Fluff ate
Mr. Cooper's special duck food.
Guess what? It was pretty good!

THINK LIKE A SCIENTIST

Peggy thinks like a scientist—and so can you!

To infer means that you use what you have noticed, or observed, to help explain how or why something happens. So, if your pet duck waddles into the kitchen with wet wings, you might infer that he just took a dip in the kiddie pool.

Look Back
Look back at page 20. What does Mr. Cooper infer about Fluff? On page 25, what does Peggy infer? What does she decide to do?

Try This!
Look closely at each picture. What can you infer?

1.   2.   3.

Possible answers include:
1. The puppy was out in the rain.
2. The baby birds are hungry.
3. The cat knocked over the vase.

32